Author Debbie Leland was at
Lake Dallas Elementary on
January 15, 2014. I bought one
of her books and she
autographed it!!

Written by
Debbie Leland

Illustrated by
Ann Hollis Rife

Wildflower Run Publishing

To: Ethan & Dylan McGovern
"Superstars!"

To my mom, Laura, and to George Gabelmann, my #1 fans.
Thanks for all your love and support– D.L.

In memory of my father, Burtis Hollis, who raised me to love football.
And to my other favorite football fan, my husband, Wayne– A.H.R.

A special thank you to Chuck and Nicki Bray.

First Edition, 2014
Text copyright © 2014 by Debbie Leland
Illustration copyright © 2014 by Ann Hollis Rife

10 9 8 7 6 5 4 3 2 1

Publisher's Cataloging-In-Publication data:
Leland, Debbie. The football man / Debbie Leland ; illustrated by Ann Hollis Rife. –1st ed. p. cm.
Summary: A gingerbread football man runs away from a mob of mascots until he reaches
the stadium where a rhino offers to help him cross the field.
ISBN: 978-09667086-5-3
[1.Gingerbread –Fiction. 2. Fairy Tales – Fiction. 3. Football – Fiction.
 4. Animals – Folklore.]
I. Rife, Ann Hollis ill. II. Title.
398.2 –dc22
LCCN: 2013947089

Wildflower Run Publishing
P.O. Box 9656
College Station, TX 77842

http://www.debbie-leland.com

Deep in the South where footballs spiral
through the air like the sounds of songbirds,
lived a little ol' referee and his wife. The little
ol' referee loved gingerbread and he loved football.
The little ol' referee's wife loved her husband, and she
wanted to make him a special surprise for his birthday.

She wanted to make a real gingerbread athlete, so she used icing for his helmet and candies for his cleats. She used coconut for the gridiron, pretzel sticks for goalposts, and licorice for the line of scrimmage.

Just as she put the football in his hands that gingerbread athlete jumped off the plate and shouted, "First down!" He ran out the door like he was headed to the national championships.

"Oh no! A scrambler," shouted the referee's wife. "Come back."

"Tweeeeet, tweeeeet." The referee blew his whistle.

"Hut, hut, hike," he shouted. "Run, run as fast as you can.

You can't tackle me. I'm the football man."

He ran past a bell tower. Chimes rang, and a jaguar jumped out.

"Stop, stop, you tasty treat!" shouted the jaguar. POUNCE!

The football man cut to the left, and the jaguar clocked himself instead.

"Offside!" he said. "Run, run as fast as you can.

You can't tackle me. I'm the football man."

He ran past a fountain where a crocodile swam. Splish-splash!

"Stop, stop," shouted the crocodile. "I'm gonna eat you

with one big CHOMP!"

"Unnecessary roughness!" he said. "Run, run as fast as you can.

You can't tackle me. I'm the football man."

He ran past an old oak tree. Crunch-munch, a bear and a boar lunched.

"Yummmm, dessert," shouted the bear and the boar. "Double team."

They both dove. But they both missed, and they both ate dirt instead.

"Out of bounds!" he said. "Run, run as fast as you can. You can't tackle me. I'm the football man."

He ran past a herd of bulls playing tag. The bulls looked
at each other and licked their lips. "Blitz!"
They charged. CRASH! They bulldozed into one another instead.

"20-yard penalty!" he said. "Run, run as fast as you can.

You can't tackle me. I'm the football man."

He ran past a mansion where a chicken cocked his head around a column. "Stop, stop, you quarterback sneak!" shouted the chicken. He grabbed the football man's jersey. The football man zigged. He zagged. He zinged. He left the dizzy chicken spinning in circles.

"Personal foul!" he said. "Run, run as fast as you can.

You can't tackle me. I'm the football man."

And he kept running. He ran past a prickle of porcupines playing in the park.

"Sack that snack," they shouted. "Huddle up!"

The porcupines lined up in formation. They rushed the football man.

But he stiff-armed them, and they toppled down like a set of porcupine dominoes.

"Time-out!" he said. "Run, run as fast as you can.

You can't tackle me. I'm the football man."

He ran down a ramp and into

the stadium. He noticed a rhino in the end zone.

"You can't tackle me. I ran away from a little ol' referee, his wife,

a jaguar, a crocodile, a bear, a boar, a herd of bulls, a chicken, and a prickle

of porcupines. And I can run away from you too, I can, I can. I'm the football man."

"Oh my," said the rhino. "Even if I could I wouldn't try to catch you."

The football man turned and saw the mob of mascots closing in on him.

"Jump on my tail and I'll give you a lift," the rhino offered with an innocent grin.

The football man jumped onto the rhino's tail. The rhino walked downfield.

"They might still be able to reach you," said the rhino. "Maybe you should climb onto my back." The football man jumped onto the rhino's back.

When they were midfield the rhino said, "You might fall off. Maybe you should jump onto my nose." The football man jumped onto the rhino's nose.

Just as the rhino lifted his head to snap him up, the football man flipped off the rhino's horn and shouted, "Flag on the play!" He landed on the field running.

"Fumble," the rhino mumbled.

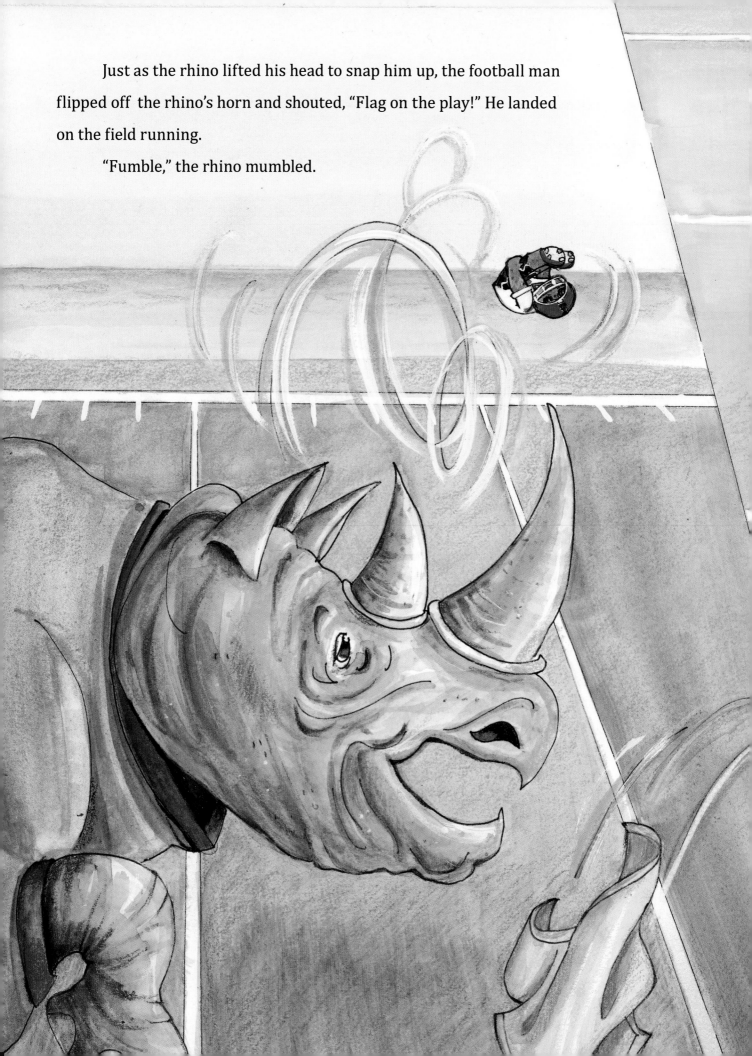

The ball bobbled up and down in his hands.

The football man grabbed the football.

He dashed. He darted. He danced around in the pocket looking for an open receiver. Defenders chased him like they were trying to tackle a jackrabbit. No one could catch him. He tucked the football by his side and ran.

As he reached the 1-yard line the defenders dove for him.
He stretched the football out in front. It crossed the goal line
just inside the pylon.

"Touchdown!" cried the little ol' referee.

The crowd cheered. The band played.

"Run, run as fast as you can," shouted the fans.

"You can't catch him. He's our superstar football man!"